THIS MAGI BOOK BELONGS TO:

_____

_____

_____

_____

For Joe
M·E·

For Roger
G·R·

Reprinted 1998 (Twice)

This paperback edition published 1997

First published in 1997 by Magi Publications
22 Manchester Street, London W1M 5PG

Text © 1997 Mark Ezra
Illustrations © 1997 Gavin Rowe

Mark Ezra and Gavin Rowe have asserted their rights
to be identified as the author and illustrator of this work
under the Copyright, Designs and Patents Act, 1988.

Printed in Belgium by Proost NV, Turnhout

ISBN 1 85430 427 5

MARK EZRA

The Frightened
Little Owl

pictures by GAVIN ROWE

Snug in a nest in the tallest tree sat Little Owl, a feathery ball with big, golden eyes. Each night she watched her mother spread her wings and glide silently over the treetops to hunt for food.

Little Owl always felt alone and afraid as she waited for her mother to come home. All she could hear outside her nest was the rustling of the branches and the howling wind.

The world seemed a cold and frightening place.
Little Owl tugged at the soft lining of the nest
with her beak and wrapped it close around her.
It made her feel safe.

"You'll soon be able to fly like me," said Little Owl's
mother one day. "Just imagine how wonderful it will
feel when you can soar silently in the night with the
wind beneath your wings!"
"But I don't *want* to fly," cried Little Owl. "It's scary
out there. I want to stay here in my nest for ever."
And she nestled down into the hole again.

"Come with me, Little Owl," said Mother Owl
one evening. "Come and choose your own supper
tonight. You'll enjoy that!"
Little Owl scrambled out after her mother on to
a branch, but when she saw how far it was to the
ground she felt dizzy.
"I *never* want to fly!" Little Owl cried, as she edged
her way back into the nest.
And Mother Owl flew
off alone.

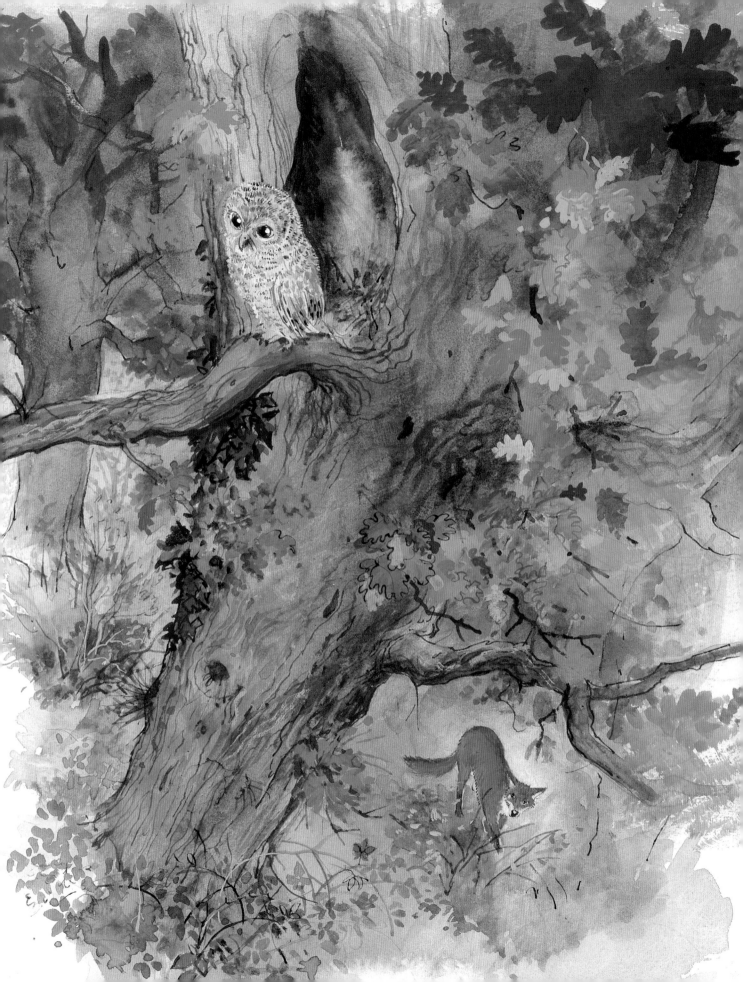

Little Owl snuggled down and waited for her supper. Outside in the wood the sun set and the moon came out. Little Owl began to feel hungry, but there was no sign of her mother. Surely she should have been back by now?

Little Owl was very worried.
What if something awful had
happened to her mother?

Little Owl plucked up all her courage and hopped out on to the branch. Somehow she felt less dizzy than she had before and the ground didn't seem so far away. Trembling, she took another step . . .

. . . and at that moment a terrific
gust of wind sprang up and Little Owl
lost her footing.

The next thing she knew she was tumbling through the air. Without thinking, she spread her wings –

and suddenly she was flying!
Flapping madly, Little Owl tried to reach her own branch, but the wind was too strong and she was buffeted to earth.

"Ouch!" cried Little Owl,
as she hit the ground.
"Well, that wasn't bad for a beginner," said
a voice nearby. "Why don't you try again?"
Little Owl looked up and saw a young fawn.
"I don't *want* to fly," cried Little Owl.
"I want my mum! She's flown away
and I'm scared that she won't
come back!"
"I bet she will," said the fawn.
"If you listen, you'll hear her."

And sure enough, from far away across the trees,
Little Owl heard a familiar sound.
"Kiew! Kiew!"

"Yes, that's her!" cried Little Owl in excitement
and saying goodbye to the fawn, she ran and
flapped across the glade.

"Mum! Mum!" cried Little Owl and before she
knew it she was flying!
"Well done!" the fawn called out, as Little Owl
rose higher and higher into the air.

Little Owl flew on, but her mother always seemed to be just ahead of her.

"Mum! Mum!" sobbed Little Owl. "Wait for me! Don't fly off again." She began to feel she would never catch up.

In her hurry and fright Little Owl bumped into
a tree. She fell to the ground, disturbing a family
of mice out for their supper.
"Run!" screamed Mother Mouse to her babies.
"Run, it's an owl!"
There was a scuffle
of tiny paws and
the mice vanished.

It was very quiet in the wood now and Little Owl
felt dreadfully alone. She gave a small sob. Perhaps
her mum had gone away for ever?
"MUM," she shrieked, "MUM WHERE ARE YOU?"
"I'm right here," said a familiar voice from above
Little Owl's head. "You didn't really think
I would leave you, did you? I've been
watching over you all the time,
hoping you would fly.
And now you can.
Well done, Little Owl!"

Little Owl blinked. Yes, she *could* fly!
She gave a hoot of delight, spread her wings and flew round and round the glade. She dipped and soared towards the morning sky. Mum was right! Flying *was* wonderful!

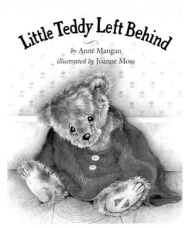
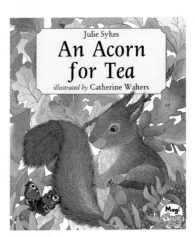

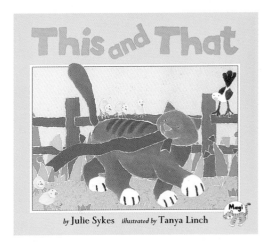